Rebus Treasury

Published by Bell Books
Boyds Mills Press, Inc.
A Highlights Company
815 Church Street
Honesdale, Pennsylvania 18431

Printed in the United States of America

Publisher Cataloging-In-Publication Data
　　　　Rebus Treasury/Compiled by the editors of Highlights for
Children
48 p.: ill.; cm.
Summary: A collection of forty-four stories, each combining words
and pictures to create a story. The plots are light and amusing.
ISBN 1-56397-777-X
1. Children's stories. 2. Picture books. I. Highlights for Children.
II. Title
813.54-dc20　　　　　　[E]　　　　1991
Library of Congress Catalog Card Number 90-85899

First Boyds Mills Press paperback edition, 1999

Weekly Reader is a registered trademark of the Weekly Reader Corporation
2005 Edition

Cover design by Ed Miller

Cover art by Doug Cushman

Contents

Reading a Rebus

Right from the start, your young child can delight in reading these rebus stories simply by identifying the little pictures. Each picture is followed by the word it represents, so your child will become familiar with the words while enjoying successful reading.

As you read these stories aloud, you may want to encourage your child to point to the pictures. Learning to follow a story by moving from left to right gives a child an important head start on the road to good reading.

We hope that the stories in this book will provide hours of family fun and help your child become a skilled, enthusiastic reader.

The Perfect Book For Bear

By Judith Ross Enderle

Illustrated by Doug Cushman

Bear wanted a book. He went to the library. He looked at books about cats. He looked at books about dogs. He looked at books about ducks. He looked at books about frogs.

"May I help you, Bear?" asked Miss Turtle, the librarian.

"I want a book," said Bear. "But I do not want a book about cats or dogs or ducks or frogs."

"I have a book for you," said Miss Turtle. "A book about boys and girls."

"Perfect," said Bear.

5

Tell Us, Turtle

By Ann Jensen

Illustrated by Olivia H.H. Cole

"April is my favorite month," said Turtle.

"Why?" asked Robin from her nest. "Is it because flowers will bloom soon?"

"I like flowers, but that is not the reason," said Turtle.

"Is it because the breezes are soft and warm?" asked Squirrel.

"I like soft, warm breezes," said Turtle. "But that is not the reason."

"Is it because the grass is fresh and green?" Bunny asked.

"I like fresh, green grass," said Turtle. "But that is not the reason."

"What is the reason then?" asked Robin.

"Yes, tell us," said Squirrel and Bunny.

"April is my favorite month because there are April showers, and I like the sound of rain on my roof," said Turtle.

6

The Puddle

By Virginia Choo
Illustrated by Sue Parnell

The rain came down hard. Red Rooster put up his red umbrella to keep off the rain. Blue Snake put up her blue umbrella. Green Turtle put up his green umbrella. Orange Butterfly put up her orange umbrella. Pink Pig put up his pink umbrella.

Then the rain stopped. Red Rooster closed his red umbrella. Blue Snake closed her blue umbrella. Green Turtle closed his green umbrella. Orange Butterfly closed her orange umbrella. Pink Pig closed his pink umbrella.

The rain made a big puddle. Red Rooster opened his red umbrella and sailed across. Blue Snake opened her blue umbrella and sailed across. Green Turtle opened his green umbrella and sailed across. Orange Butterfly flew over the big puddle. Pink Pig looked at the big puddle and jumped right in!

7

Dana's Farm Friends

By Betty Ann Porter

Illustrated by Meryl Henderson

"I don't have any friends to play with," said Dana.

"Go look around the farm," said Grandma. "Take some crackers and apples with you for a snack."

In the barn Dana found a kitten. She petted the kitten and talked to it. When Dana left the barn, the kitten followed quietly behind her.

At the pond Dana saw a duck. She threw some crackers to the duck. The duck waddled out of the pond and followed behind the kitten.

Next Dana saw a pony munching hay. She patted the pony and gave him an apple.

Dana walked back to the house, and the pony trotted behind the duck.

Just then Dana saw what was following her—a kitten, a duck, and a pony!

"I have friends I didn't even know about!" shouted Dana.

Willie's Wagon

By Shirley Markham Jorjorian

Illustrated by Neva Shultz

Willie helped Mother and Father unpack.

"I like our new house," said Willie. "But I wish I had some friends."

"You will make new friends soon," said Mother. "Here, take this box out to the trash can."

Willie took the box outside. He saw a piece of rope. He tied the rope to the box.

He drew wheels on the box.

"Now I have a wagon," said Willie.

"Will you let my little doll have a ride?" asked a girl.

"Sure," said Willie. He pulled the wagon down the street.

Then children came from everywhere, carrying pets and teddy bears. Willie forgot that his wagon used to be a box. He had new friends.

9

Something New

By Judith Ross Enderle

Illustrated by Dev Appleyard

Lee and Grandpa were walking in the garden. Grandpa stopped by the pond. "Let's feed the fish," he said.

Lee looked into the pond. "I see my face," he said, "but I do not see any fish."

"I will call the fish," Grandpa said. He touched the water with his hand. He made little waves. Five fish swam into sight. Grandpa took bread from his pocket. He handed it to Lee. They threw little pieces of bread to the fish.

"Why did the fish come when you made waves?" Lee asked.

"The fish have learned that when I touch the water, it is time to eat," Grandpa said.

"I know that my dog can learn," Lee said. "But I did not know that fish could learn. That is something new."

"It is a good day when you learn something new," Grandpa said.

The Three Tadpoles

By Carolyn Ezell

Illustrated by Linda Weller

 John and  Mother caught  three  tadpoles in a lake. They put the  three  tadpoles into a  pail of lake water.

"What are  tadpoles?" asked  John. "Are they baby  fish?"

"Wait and see," said  Mother. "We will watch them grow."

 John fed the  tadpoles a little turtle food every day. Maybe my  tadpoles are baby turtles, he thought.

The  tadpoles grew bigger and bigger. In a few weeks they had  legs. Their  tails grew shorter and shorter.

 Mother poured most of the water out of the  pail.

 John put in a  rock that stuck up out of the water. HOP! HOP! HOP! went the  tadpoles one day.

 "Mother!" called  John. "Now I know what  tadpoles are." HOP! HOP! HOP! "Look! My  tadpoles have turned into  frogs!"

11

Ant and Beetle

By Marileta Robinson

Illustrated by Sue Parnell

"Let's play follow-the-leader," said  Ant. "I will be leader."

Ant climbed over a stick. Beetle climbed over the stick. Ant crawled under a leaf. Beetle crawled under the leaf. Ant ran through a puddle. Beetle ran through the puddle. Ant climbed up a tall stalk of grass. "No, Ant," said Beetle. "That is too high for me. I cannot follow you up there."

"That is too bad, Beetle," said Ant. "It is fun to be up high."

The wind began to blow the stalk. "Whee!" said Ant. The wind blew harder. "Help!" said Ant. "I am going to fall!"

Beetle climbed up the stalk. The stalk bent lower and lower. At last it touched the ground.

"Thank you, Beetle," said Ant. "I am glad we are friends."

"I am glad, too," said Beetle.

Something Exciting

By Caroline Arnold

Illustrated by Sue Parnell

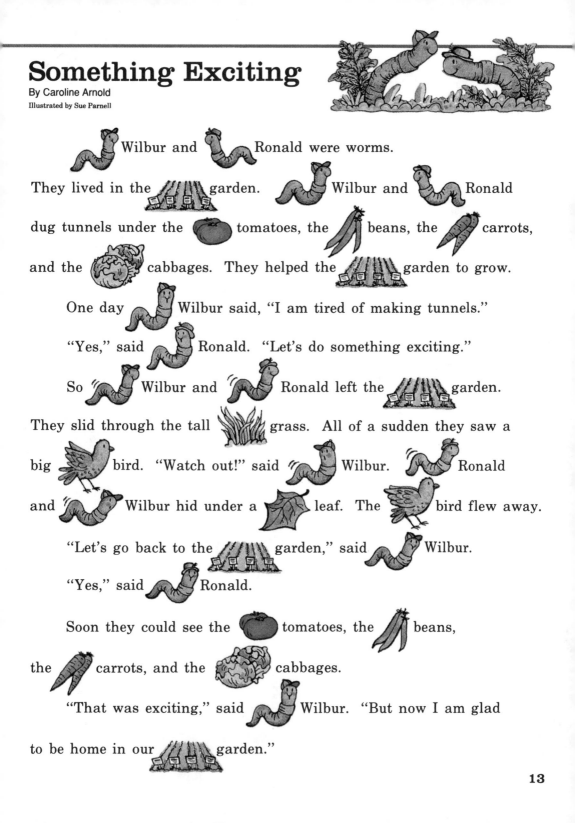

Wilbur and Ronald were worms.

They lived in the garden. Wilbur and Ronald

dug tunnels under the tomatoes, the beans, the carrots,

and the cabbages. They helped the garden to grow.

One day Wilbur said, "I am tired of making tunnels."

"Yes," said Ronald. "Let's do something exciting."

So Wilbur and Ronald left the garden.

They slid through the tall grass. All of a sudden they saw a

big bird. "Watch out!" said Wilbur. Ronald

and Wilbur hid under a leaf. The bird flew away.

"Let's go back to the garden," said Wilbur.

"Yes," said Ronald.

Soon they could see the tomatoes, the beans,

the carrots, and the cabbages.

"That was exciting," said Wilbur. "But now I am glad

to be home in our garden."

13

Jungle Action

By Sally Lucas

Illustrated by Mij Colson-Barnum

A  plant in the jungle was on  fire.

 "Fire!" called a  monkey to a  lion.

 "Fire!" roared the  lion to a  tiger.

 "Fire!" growled the  tiger to an  elephant.

The  elephant stuck his  trunk into a  puddle of water. The  elephant sprayed the burning  plant with his  trunk. Out went the  fire.

"Safe!" called the  monkey to the  lion.

"Safe!" roared the  lion to the  tiger.

"Safe!" growled the  tiger to the  elephant.

"Thirsty!" said the  elephant to himself. Then the  elephant went looking for another  puddle of water!

The Jungle Band

By Sandra Steen and Susan Steen

Illustrated by Mij Colson-Barnum

One afternoon in the jungle 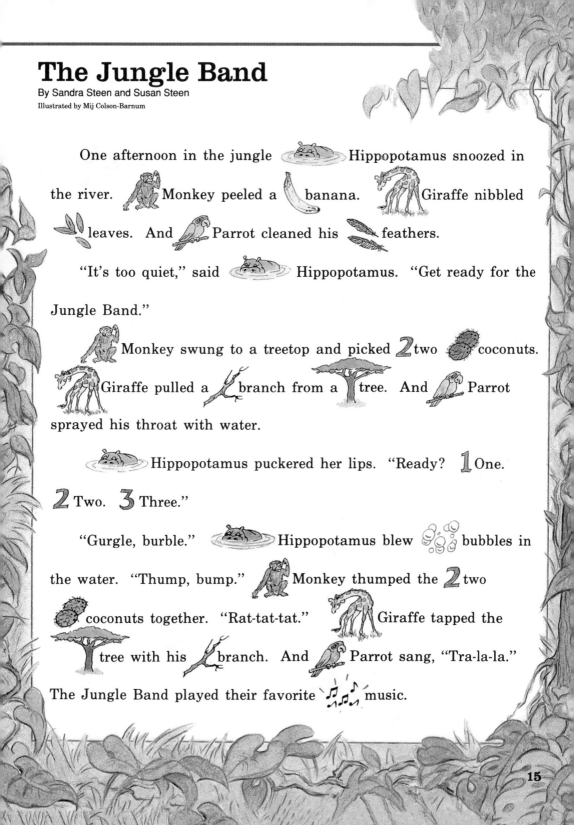 Hippopotamus snoozed in the river. Monkey peeled a banana. Giraffe nibbled leaves. And Parrot cleaned his feathers.

"It's too quiet," said Hippopotamus. "Get ready for the Jungle Band."

Monkey swung to a treetop and picked 2 two coconuts. Giraffe pulled a branch from a tree. And Parrot sprayed his throat with water.

Hippopotamus puckered her lips. "Ready? 1 One. 2 Two. 3 Three."

"Gurgle, burble." Hippopotamus blew bubbles in the water. "Thump, bump." Monkey thumped the 2 two coconuts together. "Rat-tat-tat." Giraffe tapped the tree with his branch. And Parrot sang, "Tra-la-la." The Jungle Band played their favorite music.

Circus Jobs!

By Marilyn Kratz

Illustrated by Jerome Weisman

"What would you be if you joined the circus?"

Mrs. Archer asked her class one day.

"I would be a lion tamer," said Joshua. "I would teach the lions to jump and roar."

"I would be a clown," said Rachel. "I would make the children laugh."

"I would be an acrobat," said Philip. "I would swing high over the crowd."

"It would be fun to be a lion tamer or a clown or an acrobat," said Dustin. "But I would not be any of those. I know another important job."

"What job would you like to have?" asked Mrs. Archer.

"I would drive the truck that brings the circus to our town," said Dustin.

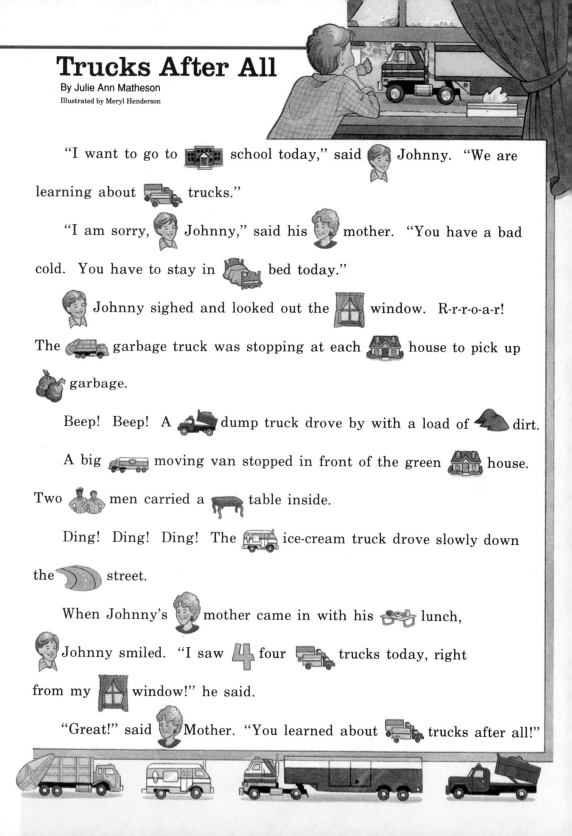

Trucks After All

By Julie Ann Matheson

Illustrated by Meryl Henderson

"I want to go to 🏫 school today," said 👦 Johnny. "We are learning about 🚚 trucks."

"I am sorry, 👦 Johnny," said his 👩 mother. "You have a bad cold. You have to stay in 🛏 bed today."

👦 Johnny sighed and looked out the 🪟 window. R-r-r-o-a-r! The 🚛 garbage truck was stopping at each 🏠 house to pick up 🗑 garbage.

Beep! Beep! A 🚚 dump truck drove by with a load of 🟫 dirt.

A big 🚚 moving van stopped in front of the green 🏠 house. Two 👷👷 men carried a 🪑 table inside.

Ding! Ding! Ding! The 🚐 ice-cream truck drove slowly down the 🛣 street.

When Johnny's 👩 mother came in with his 🍽 lunch, 👦 Johnny smiled. "I saw 4 four 🚚 trucks today, right from my 🪟 window!" he said.

"Great!" said 👩 Mother. "You learned about 🚚 trucks after all!"

Sam Goes to the Supermarket

By Arline Rose

Illustrated by Ethel Gold

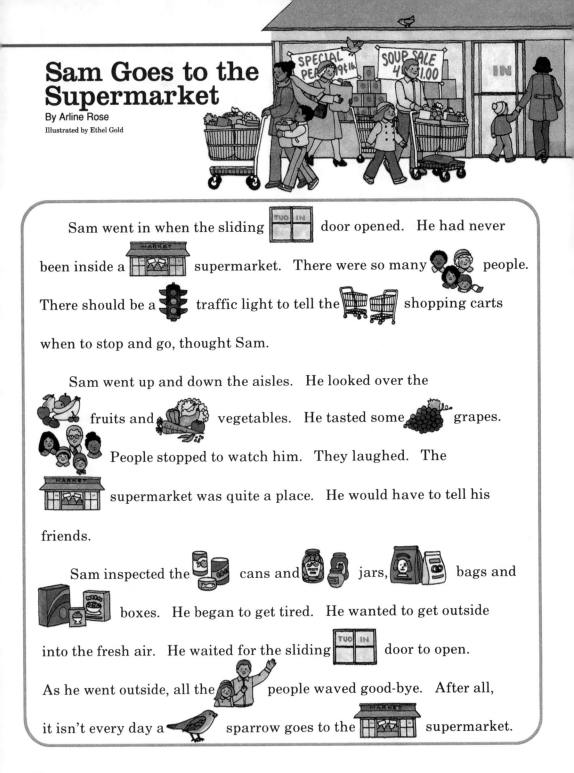

Sam went in when the sliding door opened. He had never been inside a supermarket. There were so many people. There should be a traffic light to tell the shopping carts when to stop and go, thought Sam.

Sam went up and down the aisles. He looked over the fruits and vegetables. He tasted some grapes. People stopped to watch him. They laughed. The supermarket was quite a place. He would have to tell his friends.

Sam inspected the cans and jars, bags and boxes. He began to get tired. He wanted to get outside into the fresh air. He waited for the sliding door to open. As he went outside, all the people waved good-bye. After all, it isn't every day a sparrow goes to the supermarket.

18

Lion Goes Shopping

By Pat Relf

Illustrated by Cynthia Amrine

One day  Lion said, "I need some things at the store."

So Lion and Tiger went shopping. Lion pushed the cart. He and Tiger walked up and down the aisles, looking at bananas, peas, and eggs. They saw brooms and books. Lion didn't put anything in the cart.

Tiger was getting tired. "We have walked up and down every aisle, and your cart is still empty, Lion," he said. "I thought you needed to buy something at the store."

"I did," said Lion. "But I can't remember what I needed. It wasn't bananas or eggs or books. I just can't remember!"

"Next time you should make a list," said Tiger. "Write down the things you need so you won't forget them."

"That's it!" said Lion. "Thank you, Tiger. I needed to buy some paper and pencils for making a list!"

Responsibility Kitten

By Stephanie Gordon Tessler

Illustrated by Sue Parnell

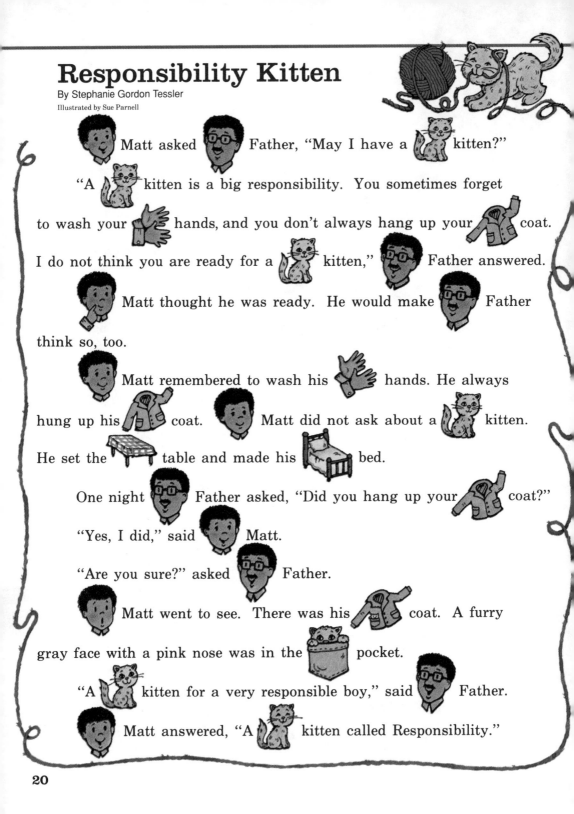

Matt asked Father, "May I have a kitten?"

"A kitten is a big responsibility. You sometimes forget to wash your hands, and you don't always hang up your coat. I do not think you are ready for a kitten," Father answered.

Matt thought he was ready. He would make Father think so, too.

Matt remembered to wash his hands. He always hung up his coat. Matt did not ask about a kitten. He set the table and made his bed.

One night Father asked, "Did you hang up your coat?"

"Yes, I did," said Matt.

"Are you sure?" asked Father.

Matt went to see. There was his coat. A furry gray face with a pink nose was in the pocket.

"A kitten for a very responsible boy," said Father.

Matt answered, "A kitten called Responsibility."

20

Pig Practices

By Judith Ross Enderle

Illustrated by Cynthia Amrine

 Pig sat at the piano. "My new music is hard," he said. "I think I will ride my bike."

But first Pig played **3** three notes on the piano.

"Or maybe I will play with my truck."

Then Pig played **3** three more notes on the piano.

"Or I could eat an apple."

He played **6** six notes on the piano.

"This new music is still hard," Pig said.

He played **6** six more notes and still more notes after that. Soon the new music was not so hard.

Then Pig ate an apple, played with his truck, and rode his bike.

Sally's Supermarket Visit

By Pat Padams

Illustrated by C.S. Ewing

One day  Sally wanted to go shopping with Father.

"I have a long list of groceries to buy," Father said.

"I can help you," Sally said. "I can push the cart."

"You are too little," said Father, "but you may come along."

At the store Sally watched Father put milk and eggs into the cart. Then they went to the fresh fruit section.

"We need 10 ten apples," Father said.

"I can count to 10 ten," Sally said. She put 10 ten apples into a bag.

In the canned food section, Father looked and looked for a can of corn. Sally found one on the bottom shelf.

"I did not look down there," said Father with a smile.

"Am I helping you?" Sally asked.

Father nodded. "You are a big help," he said. "I think you are big enough to push the cart after all."

Sara's Ribbons

By Sally Lucas

Illustrated by Olivia H.H. Cole

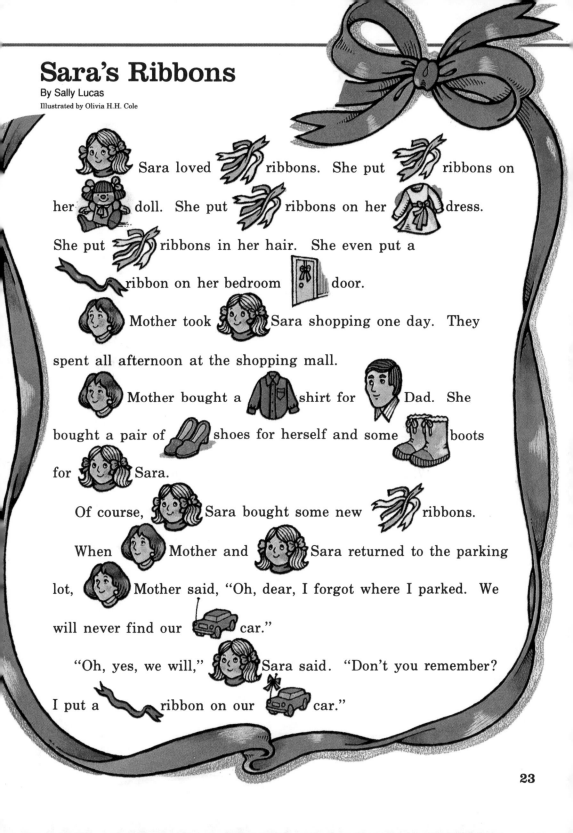

Sara loved ribbons. She put ribbons on her doll. She put ribbons on her dress. She put ribbons in her hair. She even put a ribbon on her bedroom door.

Mother took Sara shopping one day. They spent all afternoon at the shopping mall.

Mother bought a shirt for Dad. She bought a pair of shoes for herself and some boots for Sara.

Of course, Sara bought some new ribbons.

When Mother and Sara returned to the parking lot, Mother said, "Oh, dear, I forgot where I parked. We will never find our car."

"Oh, yes, we will," Sara said. "Don't you remember? I put a ribbon on our car."

Berta's Adventure

By Mark and Donna Hicks

Illustrated by Jan Pyk

One day when  Berta was drawing a picture of the clouds, her pencil turned into a big, yellow balloon. Berta floated up among the birds and the clouds.

Suddenly her pencil turned into a rocket, and Berta zoomed toward the moon and a star beyond.

While Berta was flying in space, a star turned into a starfish in an ocean of blue, and her pencil turned into a little yellow boat.

Berta was ready to set sail for another fun adventure, but first Berta had to sharpen her pencil.

The Best Way to Travel

By Stephanie Moody

Illustrated by Cathy Beylon

"Do you want to go to the park today?" Matt asked his new neighbor Sara.

"That is a good idea," Sara said. "But how will we get there?"

"We could ride our bicycles," Matt answered. "Or we could ride in my wagon."

Sara smiled. Then she said, "If the park were across town, we could go on the bus."

"How about riding in a big airplane?" asked Matt. "If the park were around the world, we could do that."

"Just imagine," said Sara. "If the park were on the moon, we could ride in a rocket ship."

"That would be fun," said Matt. "But the park is not on the moon. It is not even across town. It is only around the corner."

"Then I know the best way to get there," Sara said. "We can walk on our very own feet." And they did.

25

Barney Packs His Suitcase

By Marlys G. Stapelbroek

Illustrated by Joseph Ewers

Barney was going to visit Grandmother Bear. Barney's mother carried a big suitcase into his room. "It's time to pack," she told Barney.

Barney opened the suitcase. It looked big enough to carry everything he would need at Grandmother's house.

First Barney put in his favorite blanket. Next he packed his red truck. Then he packed his rabbit, Freddy. He put in 6 six books to read at bedtime. There was just enough room for some paper and crayons on top.

"I'm all packed," Barney told mother proudly.

Mother looked in the suitcase. "But, Barney, you didn't pack any clothes!"

Barney looked surprised. "I guess this suitcase isn't big enough after all!"

Jay's Three Good Guesses

By Elaine M. Marshall

Illustrated by Meryl Henderson

Grandpa talked to Jay on the telephone.

"There is a surprise waiting for you at the airport," said Grandpa. "I'll give you **3** three chances to guess what the surprise could be."

"I like guessing games," said Jay.

"Does the surprise like to read books about animals?" asked Jay.

"Yes," said Grandpa.

"Does the surprise like to feed ducks at the park?" asked Jay.

"Yes," said Grandpa.

"Does the surprise like to play guessing games?" asked Jay.

"Yes, indeed," said Grandpa.

"I know what the surprise is. It's you, Grandpa!" shouted Jay.

"You're right." Grandpa laughed.

The Mother Gooseland Fair

By Sally Lucas   Illustrated by Lynn Adams

Mother Hubbard went to her cupboard to fetch her homemade bread. The bread wasn't there. Mother Hubbard asked everywhere, "Who took my homemade bread?"

"Not I," said her kitten. "I've been looking for my mitten."

"Not I," said Bo-Peep. "I've been looking for my sheep."

"Not I," said Miss Muffet. "I've been sitting on my tuffet."

"Not I," said Jack Horner. "I've been sitting in a corner."

The little dog said, "I took your bread to the Mother Gooseland Fair. It was the winner. Old King Cole ate it for dinner. He called it the best bread there."

Mother Hubbard proudly went to her cupboard and hung her blue ribbon there.

The Missing Teddy

By T. Casler Mallory

Illustrated by Laurie Jordan

"I can't find my teddy bear," said Rebekah one day after coming home from the park.

"Did you leave him by the swings?" asked Mother.

"No." Rebekah shook her head. "Not at the swings."

"What about the merry-go-round?" suggested Dad.

"No, I don't think I left him on the merry-go-round," said Rebekah.

"We'll go back after dinner to look for him," said Mother.

Rebekah went to her room. She looked at her bed. There were her bunny, her dolls, a furry elephant, her giraffe, and her teddy bear.

Rebekah ran to tell Mother and Dad.

"Now I remember," she said. "I left my teddy bear at home so he wouldn't get lost."

"That was a good idea," Dad said.

"A very good idea," agreed Mother.

Why It Rains

By Judith Ross Enderle

Illustrated by Kit Wray

One day Stevie looked out the window.

"Why does it rain?" he asked Dad.

"It rains so flowers will grow," said Dad.

"Why else?" asked Stevie.

"So trees will get washed," said Dad.

"Why else?" asked Stevie.

"So we will have water to drink," said Dad.

"Why else?" asked Stevie.

"So the sun can make more clouds," said Dad.

"Why else?" asked Stevie.

"I do not know why else," said Dad.

"So I can wear my boots and carry my big blue umbrella," said Stevie.

"I should have thought of that," said Dad.

What's in the Garden?

By Rosella J. Schroeder

Illustrated by Sue Parnell

One sunny day Ruth and Randy went out to the garden.

They used a rake to smooth the soil and made straight rows with a hoe.

Ruth planted green beans, corn, and carrots.

Randy planted beets, pumpkins, and lettuce.

As they worked, a big cloud filled the sky. Lightning flashed and it thundered. Rain began to fall.

The children took the rake and the hoe and ran to the house. It began to pour. It was still raining when Ruth and Randy went to bed that night.

In the morning Randy said, "Look. Our garden is covered with water. The creek has overflowed because of the rain."

Ruth said, "There are ducks swimming in our garden."

"What a surprise," she said. "Where we planted carrots and beets, pumpkins and lettuce, corn and green beans, we got ducks."

31

Three in a Tree

By Judith Ross Enderle

Illustrated by Cathy Beylon

There was a 🌳 tree. In the 🌳 tree there were **3** three—a 🐦 bird, a 🐝 bee, and 👧 Emmy Lee. That's me.

The 🐦 bird built a 🪺 nest in the top of the 🌳 tree. The 🐝 bee buzzed at 🌸 flowers in the middle of the 🌳 tree. And I built a 🏠 house in the bottom of the 🌳 tree—a treehouse for me.

The 🐦 bird left her 🪺 nest. She chased the 🐝 bee. The 🐝 bee left her 🌸 flowers. She chased me. And I fell out of my 🏠 house in the 🌳 tree. There were no longer **3** three in the 🌳 tree.

The 🐦 bird flew away from her 🪺 nest in the top of the 🌳 tree. The 🐝 bee flew away from her 🌸 flowers in the middle of the 🌳 tree. That left just me.

So I called **2** two friends to come and see the 🏠 house I had built in the bottom of the 🌳 tree. Now once again there are **3** three in a 🌳 tree— 👧 Tracy and 👦 Tony and 👧 Emmy Lee. That's me.

Leaf Shapes

By Stephanie Moody   Illustrated by Lorraine Arthur

 Mark and  Kate were walking through the forest. The ☀ sun sparkled in the sky.

"Let's have some fun," said  Mark. "Let's find  leaves that are different shapes."

"I see a big  leaf,"  Kate said. "It looks like a ♥ heart."

"There is a  leaf like a ✳ star,"  Mark said. "And there is another  leaf that looks like a  feather from a  bird."

"Look,"  Kate said. "This  leaf is shaped like my  hand when I spread my fingers apart."

"See this," said  Mark. "This  leaf is the best shape of all."

"What shape is it?" asked  Kate.

"It is  leaf shaped," said  Mark.

The North Wind and the Sun

Based on a Fable by Aesop Retold by Mavis Catalfio

Illustrated by Katharine Dodge

One day the  North Wind told the  Sun, "I am much stronger than you."

"No," said the  Sun. "I am stronger. I will show you. See the  boy walking along the  road? Can you take his  coat away?"

The  North Wind laughed. "That is easy!" he said. He blew on the  boy. The  boy shivered and pulled his  coat closer around him. The  North Wind blew harder. The  boy held his  coat even tighter. The  North Wind could not blow the.  coat off the  boy.

"Now it is my turn," said the  Sun. The  Sun shone on the  boy. The  boy let his  coat hang loose around him. The  Sun grew warmer. The  boy took off his  coat and skipped down the  road.

The gentle  Sun had won the quarrel.

Runaway Kite

By Elaine Pageler

Illustrated by Roberta Langman

Little  Kite wanted to run away. It went up over a  tree.

"Go home," said the  tree.

"No," said Little  Kite. It headed for a  hill.

"Go home," said the  hill.

"No," said Little  Kite. It raced up to a  cloud.

"Go home," said the  cloud.

"No," said Little  Kite. It soared over the  rainbow.

"Go home," said the  rainbow.

"No," said Little  Kite. It dived at a  boy.

"Come home," said the  boy and tugged on its string.

"Yes," said Little  Kite and flew to the ground.

Mouse Manners

By Sally Lucas

Illustrated by Cynthia Amrine

A  mouse saw a little

 house. "What a nice  house," said the  mouse.

The  mouse opened the front  door and went inside.

The  mouse saw a little  chair. "What a

nice  chair," said the  mouse. The  mouse sat

in the  chair. The  mouse rocked back and

forth. "I like this  house," said the  mouse.

"So do I," said a  doll. "This is my  house. You

are sitting in my  chair."

The  mouse jumped out of the  chair. "I didn't

know it was your  house," said the  mouse. "I

will leave."

"You don't have to leave," said the  doll. "You just have

to learn to knock on the  door before you come in. Even in

a dollhouse, a  mouse must have manners."

36

Three Mice on a Skateboard

By Sally Lucas   Illustrated by Liisa Chauncy Guida

Three mice lived in a toy house. The first mouse sat on a roller skate. "Push me," said the first mouse to the other mice. After a push, the skate took the first mouse for a ride in the toy house.

The second mouse sat on a toy truck. "Push me," said the second mouse to the other mice. The toy truck took the second mouse for a ride in the toy house.

The third mouse sat on a skateboard. Along came a cat. The first and second mice jumped on the skateboard, too. "Push us," said the three mice to the cat.

The cat gave the skateboard a push. "Wheee," cried the three mice as the skateboard slid right out of the house. "This is the best ride of all. It takes us away from the cat!"

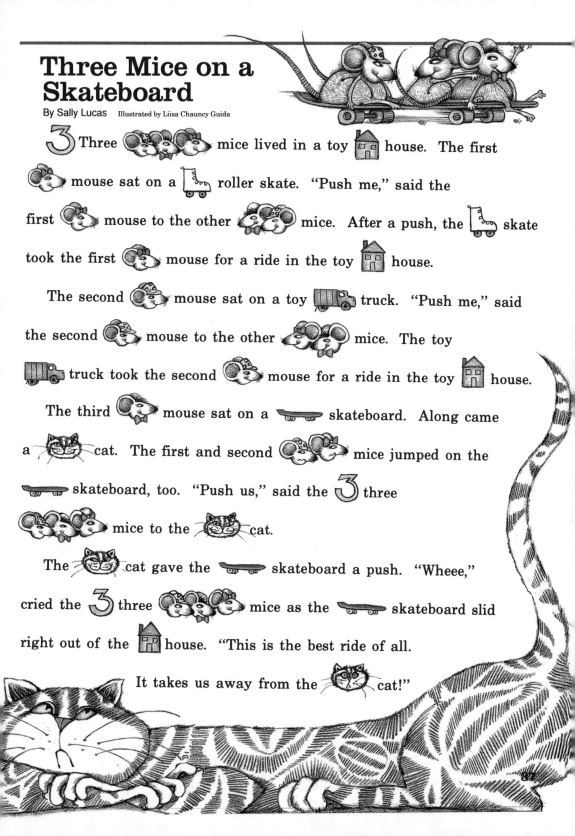

Danny's Mother's Shoes

By Toby Speed

Illustrated by Roberta Collier

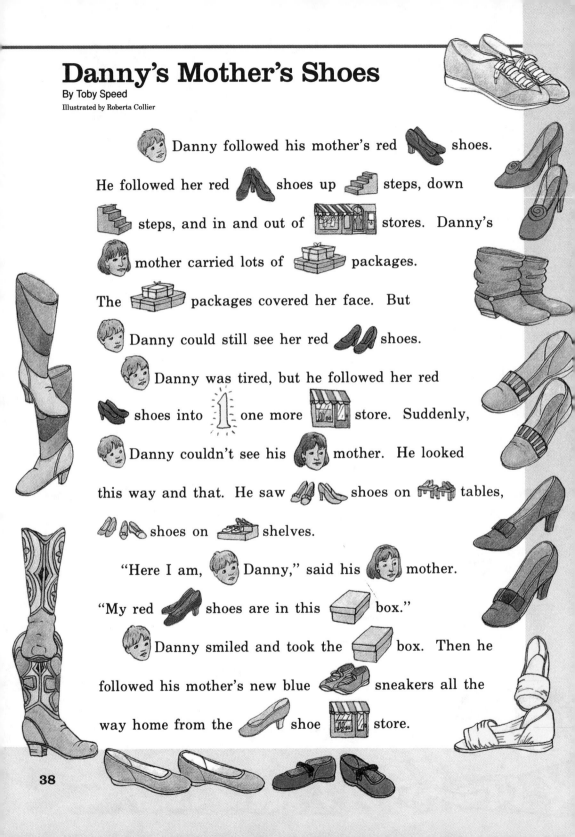

Danny followed his mother's red shoes.

He followed her red shoes up steps, down steps, and in and out of stores. Danny's mother carried lots of packages. The packages covered her face. But Danny could still see her red shoes.

Danny was tired, but he followed her red shoes into one more store. Suddenly, Danny couldn't see his mother. He looked this way and that. He saw shoes on tables, shoes on shelves.

"Here I am, Danny," said his mother. "My red shoes are in this box."

Danny smiled and took the box. Then he followed his mother's new blue sneakers all the way home from the shoe store.

38

George's Goat

By Kent Brown Jr.

Illustrated by Meryl Henderson

George had a little goat. The goat lived outside with the cows.

When George went to the barn, the goat went, too. When George walked over the bridge, so did the goat. When George went into the house, the goat had to wait outside.

One morning George got ready for school. He put on his jacket. He picked up his lunch box. He walked over the bridge. The goat came along. He walked to the road. So did the goat.

Soon the bus came. The door of the bus opened, and George got on. The goat got on the bus, too.

The door of the bus opened again. George carried the goat off the bus. "I am sorry," he said. "A goat cannot go to school."

Blocks and Baby Brothers

By Judith Ross Enderle   Illustrated by Olivia H.H. Cole

Iris emptied her whole box of blocks onto the floor. She began to build a tower.

Ben, her baby brother, knocked the tower down.

"Please do not do that, Ben." said Iris. "Play with your bear or your ball."

Iris began to build another tower.

Ben did not play with his bear. He did not play with his ball. Ben watched. Then he knocked the tower down.

Iris had a good idea. She got a small box. She put six blocks in the box.

"These are your blocks," she told Ben. She showed her brother how to build a tower.

Iris played with her blocks. Ben did not bother her. He was too busy with his blocks.

Mama's Mop

By Sandra Steen and Susan Steen

Illustrated by Pat Stewart

JoJo hit his spoon on his cup. "Mama, Mama."

"Mama is washing the car," Mark said. "She told me to baby-sit."

Mark looked around the kitchen. "Watch what I can do with Mama's new mop."

Mark put the mop between his legs. "This is a great big horse. I'm a cowboy." He ran around the kitchen.

JoJo clapped his hands.

Mark held up the mop. "This is a girl. I'm a dancer." He danced around the kitchen.

JoJo laughed and laughed.

Mark put the mop on a chair. "This is a lion. I'm a lion tamer." He pretended to crack a whip.

Suddenly JoJo knocked over his cup of milk.

"This is a mop," Mark said. "I'm a housekeeper." He wiped up the milk.

Sara's Wish

By T. Casler Mallory

Illustrated by Joseph Ewers

"I wish I had a  horse," Sara said one day.

"What would you do with a horse?" asked Dad.

"First, I'd put on my jeans and my checkered shirt," Sara said. "Then I'd tie a bandanna around my neck, pull on my cowboy boots, and put on my cowboy hat. Next I'd take my beautiful striped blanket and put it on the back of my horse. On top of that I'd put my saddle. Then I'd go riding."

"But, Sara, you don't have a bandanna or cowboy boots or a cowboy hat or a blanket or a saddle," Dad said.

Her blue eyes twinkled, and Sara smiled.

"That's all right, Dad," Sara said. "I don't have a horse yet, either."

42

Beth's Birthday

By Dorothy Gordon

Illustrated by Olivia H.H. Cole

Beth had wanted a puppy for a long time. She looked at her birthday packages.

"A heap of packages," she thought. "No sign of a puppy. Another birthday and still no puppy."

Dad brought in Beth's birthday cake.

"I will keep on wishing," Beth said to herself. Before she blew out the candles on the cake, she made one more wish for a puppy.

It was fun opening the packages. She liked her gifts. There was one package still to be opened.

"It is a book," Beth thought. "Dad always gives me a book."

She unwrapped the package. It was a book about how to take care of a puppy. "But I do not have a puppy," Beth said.

"Look in your room," Dad suggested.

In her room Beth found a basket. In the basket was a cuddly puppy. "My birthday wish came true!" Beth cried.

How Big a Bug?

By Marileta Robinson   Illustrated by Joseph Ewers

Bill was kicking his soccer ball against the garage. He looked at his foot.

"Yuk!" he yelled. "There's a bug on my foot!"

His twin sister Jill looked up from the book she was reading. "Is it a big bug, Bill?" she asked.

"Yes, it's big. It's a big, ugly bug!"

"Is it as big as an egg?" asked Jill.

Bill looked at the bug. "No, it's not that big," he said.

"Is it as big as a dime?" asked Jill.

"No, not that big," he said. It was climbing up his shoelace.

"Is it as big as a pea?" Jill asked.

"No, not that big."

"It doesn't sound like a very big bug," she said.

Bill shook his foot. "It is big! It's as big as . . ."

He looked at his foot. "Never mind," he said.

"It's gone."

Tim's Guessing Game

By Jean Kahny Wood   Illustrated by Cathy Beylon

Tim ran out of his house. Mike and his dog were playing together.

"Guess what I have at my house? It's little," said Tim. Mike could not guess.

Amy rode by on her new bike. "Guess what I have at my house? It smells sweet," said Tim.

"It's little," said Mike. Amy could not guess.

Tim saw Mrs. Bell climb out of her car. "Guess what I have at my house? It's soft," said Tim.

"It's little," said Mike.

"It smells sweet," said Amy. Mrs. Bell could not guess.

Just then a window opened at Tim's house.

Mike, Amy, and Mrs. Bell heard a loud noise.

"Oh!" they all said together. "We know what's little and sweet and soft and noisy. A baby!"

"Yes," said Tim. "Come see our new baby."

The Honey Tree

By Dorothy Gordon

Illustrated by Marilyn Bass

Sonny Bear was sad. Every  honey jar in the cupboard was empty. No honey for his bread. No honey for his pancakes.

"When Father Bear finds a honey tree, we will have honey," Mother Bear said.

"What a beautiful sight that must be, a tree loaded down with honey jars," Sonny Bear thought. "I will find a honey tree."

Sonny Bear walked and walked through the forest looking for a tree covered with honey jars. At last he grew tired. He sat down under a tall tree. He saw Father Bear coming. He was carrying Mother Bear's big bucket and her big spoon.

"Well, Sonny Bear," Father Bear cried. "You have found the right place."

Sonny Bear watched Father Bear climb the tree. He saw Father Bear dip honey out of a big hole in the tree.

"I am learning about honey trees," Sonny Bear thought. "A honey tree is not covered with honey jars."

That night he ate pancakes with plenty of honey.

46

Bear's New Glasses

By Pat Relf

Illustrated by Marion Krupp

"You look different today, 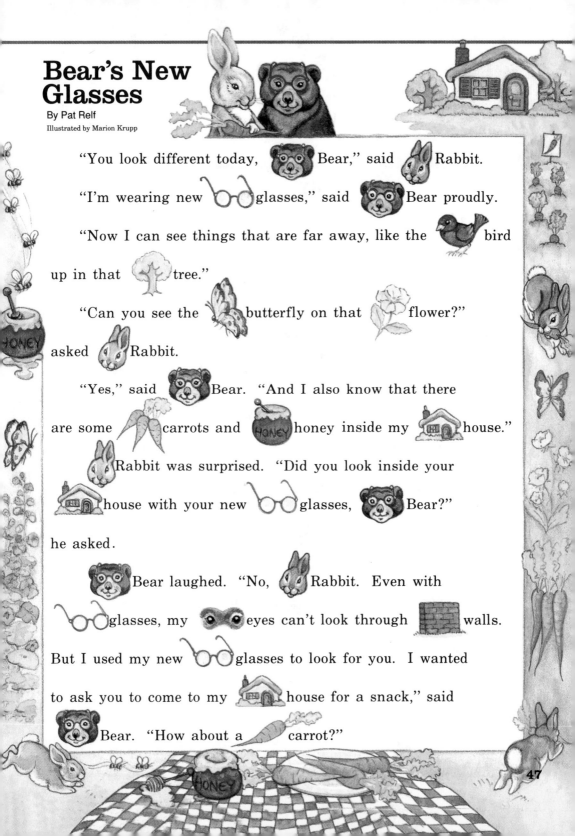 Bear," said Rabbit.

"I'm wearing new glasses," said Bear proudly.

"Now I can see things that are far away, like the bird up in that tree."

"Can you see the butterfly on that flower?" asked Rabbit.

"Yes," said Bear. "And I also know that there are some carrots and honey inside my house."

Rabbit was surprised. "Did you look inside your house with your new glasses, Bear?" he asked.

Bear laughed. "No, Rabbit. Even with glasses, my eyes can't look through walls. But I used my new glasses to look for you. I wanted to ask you to come to my house for a snack," said Bear. "How about a carrot?"

The Anxious Snowman

By Sally Lucas

Illustrated by Meryl Henderson

Snowman lived in a cabin on a mountain.

One day, Snowman stood outside his cabin and watched people on skis pass by.

I don't understand, thought Snowman. No one notices me.

Snowman went into his cabin. He came out wearing a bright red jacket and hat. People kept skiing by.

They still don't notice me, thought Snowman.

A bird noticed Snowman. The bird perched on the red hat and asked Snowman, "Why are you standing here in your new jacket and hat? You can't have fun that way."

"You're right," answered Snowman.

Snowman went into his cabin. He came out wearing skis. Snowman swooshed down the mountain.

"Look!" cried a boy. "A snowman on skis. Do you think he would like to ski with us?"

"Oh," sighed Snowman. "I thought you would never ask."